The Daddy Book

TOdd PARR

Megan Tingley Books

LITTLE, BROWN AND COMPANY

New York ~ Boston

LB 1837

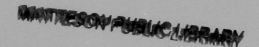

ALSO BY TODD PARR:

The Best Friends Book
Big & Little
Black & White
The Daddy Book
Do's and Don'ts
The Feel Good Book
The Feelings Book
Funny Faces
Going Places
It's Okay to Be Different
The Mommy Book
My Really Cool Baby Book
The Okay Book
Things That Make You Feel Good/
Things That Make You Feel Bad
This Is My Hair
Underwear Do's and Don'ts
Zoo Do's and Don'ts

Little, Brown and Company

Time Warner Book Group

1271 Avenue of Americas, New York, NY 10020

Visit our Web site at www.lb-kids.com

First Edition

Library of Congress Cataloging-in-Publication Data

Parr, Todd.
    The daddy book / by Todd Parr. — 1st ed.
      p. cm.
    "Megan Tingley Books"
    Summary: Represents a variety of fathers, with lots of hair and little hair,
making cookies and buying doughnuts, camping out and taking naps, and
hugging and kissing their children.
    ISBN 0-316-60799-1
    [1. Fathers — Fiction.] I. Title.
PZ7.P2447 Dad 2002
[E] — dc21   2001029097

10 9 8 7 6 5

TWP

Printed in Malaysia

This book is dedicated to
all the different kinds of dads
who have worked so hard to make
life a little bit easier with their
unconditional love and support.

Especially MY DAD!

 Love,
Todd

Some daddies take
pictures of you

Some daddies
draw pictures
of you

Some
daddies
wear
suits

Some daddies wear two different socks

Some daddies sing in the shower

Some daddies sing to you in bed

All daddies like to try

new things with you!

Some daddies work at home

Some daddies work far away

Some daddies like to build sand castles

Some daddies like to cover you with sand

Some daddies teach you how to walk

All daddies like to watch you sleep!

Some daddies have a lot of hair

Some daddies have
a little hair

Some daddies play in your tree house

Some daddies have
tea parties
with you

Some daddies make cookies

Some daddies stop for doughnuts

All daddies love to kiss

and hug you!

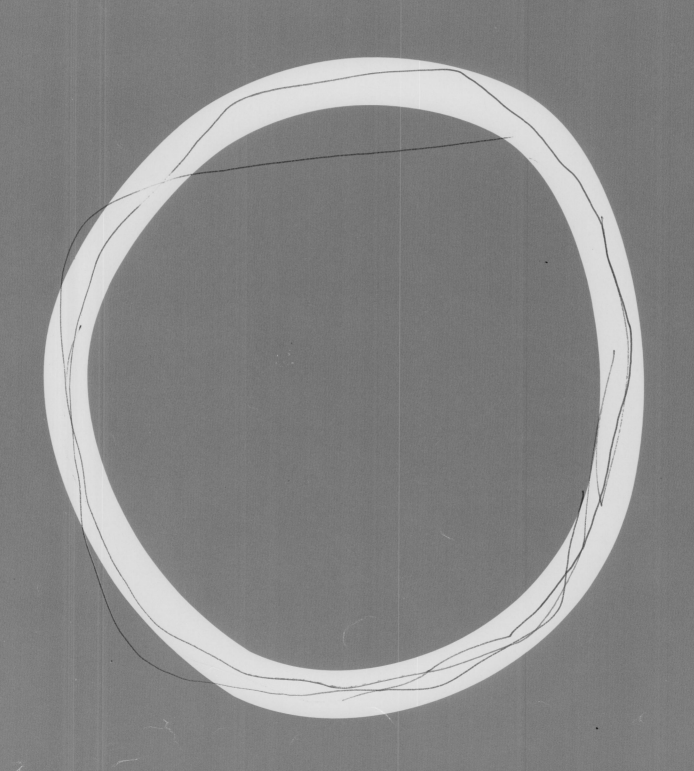

Some daddies walk you to the bus

Some daddies like to camp out with you and the dog

Some daddies like to take naps with you

All daddies want you to be who you are!